When Harry woke up on the morning
of his birthday, he found a box on his bed.
"Happy Birthday, Harry," the label
said. "With love from Mum and Dad."
Harry opened it at once.

In the box he found a cowboy hat, a waistcoat, a rope lasso, and a red hanky to tie round his neck.

"A cowboy set!" said Harry. "Wow!"

He put the outfit on over his pyjamas and went downstairs.

In the kitchen Harry's mum was reading the newspaper while his dad was frying bacon and eggs.

Harry walked in, twirling his lasso above his head.

Harry's dad almost dropped the frying pan.

"Thanks, Mum. Thanks, Dad," grinned Harry. "I'll wear these on Saturday at the Carnival. In the fancy dress parade."

"All you need now is a horse," said his mum.

After breakfast Harry dressed himself in boots and jeans and a checked shirt. He put on his cowboy outfit and walked down the street.

"Hey, Cowboy," called the milkman. "Where's your horse?"

Harry scowled and spun his lasso, just like a real cowboy.

The milkman only laughed.

Harry walked on, stamping his boots on the pavement. Coming out of the sweetshop was Ali, Harry's best friend.

"Hi, Harry," said Ali. "What you need is a horse."

"That's what everybody keeps telling me," groaned Harry.

Harry and Ali sat on the park bench, eating toffees and thinking.

"You could hire one," said Ali. "From Moon's Stables. Just for the Carnival."

Harry shook his head. "It would cost too much money," he sighed gloomily.

Ali jumped up. "Why not ask your
aunt?" he said. "The one who's a witch?"

Harry made a face. "No fear," he said.
"You never know what might happen.
We'll get turned into toads or something."

Ali pulled Harry along the street and
up the hill.

"Come on, Harry. It's your only
chance," he said.

Aunt Winnie was in the garden, stirring
something smelly in a big black pot.

"Harry!" she beamed. "I like your
outfit. All you need now is a horse."

"That's what I'm here for," said
Harry, hopefully.

Harry and Ali played with the cat while Aunt Winnie slowly turned the pages of a dusty book. They waited a long, long time.

"Got it!" cried Aunt Winnie at last. "Quick, Harry. Bring me the old wooden clothes-horse."

Harry's aunt put on her black cloak and her tall pointed hat. Then she waved her hands about and scattered some yellow powder.

"Mumbo jumbo magic force, make this turn into a horse!" she chanted.

In a flash of orange light the clothes-horse vanished. And in its place stood a huge black stallion, tossing its mane and pawing the ground.

Harry's mouth fell open in amazement and Ali dived behind a tree.

"I didn't know I could do it," beamed Aunt Winnie in delight.

Harry and Ali rode the horse proudly
home through the streets of the town.
Everybody stopped to stare.
The milkman almost fell off his cart.

"Crikey!" gulped Harry's dad. "Where are you going to keep that?"

"In the garden," said Harry. "It'll save you having to cut the grass."

"Mind it doesn't tread on my daffodils," said Harry's mum.

On Saturday morning Ali arrived very early at Harry's house. He wore a cowboy outfit, just like Harry's.

"My mum bought it for me," he grinned.

"Great!" said Harry. "Now we can ride together in the parade."

Harry and Ali spent the whole morning grooming the horse and tying ribbons in his mane.

"He's the best horse in the world," said Harry, when they had finished. "I bet we win First Prize."

19

Harry swung himself into the saddle.
Ali climbed on behind. The horse trotted
away down the street.

Harry's mum and dad stood on the
doorstep and waved.

"Ride 'em, Cowboys!" shouted the
milkman.

The town was packed with smiling people going to the Carnival. There were kings and fairies, rabbits and dragons, spacemen and clowns.

A band was playing and everybody danced in the street.

Harry and Ali joined the end of the
parade. They could see Aunt Winnie
waving at them from the crowd.

"What a handsome horse!" shouted the
milkman. Aunt Winnie beamed proudly.

Harry twirled his lasso and waved his
hat at his aunt.

And then all at once a terrible thing happened.

There was a sudden flash of orange light. Harry's horse disappeared.

Harry and Ali were flung to the ground, tangled together in the legs of Aunt Winnie's old wooden clothes-horse.

Harry said a very rude word.

Aunt Winnie helped Harry and Ali to their feet. Harry threw the clothes-horse on the rubbish bin in disgust.

"Never mind, Harry," said Aunt Winnie. "Let's go and watch the rest of the parade."

Harry and Ali and Aunt Winnie ate honey cakes and watched the parade from the balcony of Ali's flat.

"Look, Harry," said Ali. "There's Mr Moon from Moon's Stables. And just look at all his horses!"

Down the street came a team of prancing ponies. They tossed their heads and lifted their hooves in time with the music. A man in a white suit collected money in a tin.

Someone in the crowd blew a sudden loud blast on a trumpet and the ponies reared up in fright.

"Look out!" shouted Ali. "One of the ponies has bolted!"

Everybody dived out of the way as the snorting pony galloped wildly along the street.

"It's coming this way!" cried Aunt Winnie. "Quick, Harry! Grab your rope!"

Harry leaned over the balcony rail, spinning his lasso.

Harry waited until the pony was
galloping right under the balcony. Then
he dropped the noose neatly over its
head.

Ali and Aunt Winnie grabbed the rope
and they all heaved as hard as they could.

"Whoa, boy!" they shouted, as the
pony slowed to a trot.

The crowd clapped and cheered in
delight.

Harry and Ali ran down the balcony
stairs and led the pony safely back to his
master.

"Well done, boys," said Mr Moon.
"You deserve a reward."

Harry and Ali didn't win a prize in the
fancy dress parade, after all.

But Mr Moon gave them each a five
pound note, and told them they could
both ride the ponies at the Stables, any
time they liked.

And that was the best prize of all.

Harry's Horse
Sheila Lavelle

Illustrated by
Jo Davies

Hamish Hamilton
London

First published in Great Britain 1987
by Hamish Hamilton Children's Books
27 Wrights Lane, London W8 5TZ
Text copyright © 1987 by Sheila Lavelle
Illustrations copyright © 1987 by Jo Davies

British Library Cataloguing in Publication Data

Lavelle, Sheila
Harry's Horse.——(Cartwheels)
I. Title   II. Davies, Jo   III. Series
823'.914[J]   PZ7

ISBN 0–241–11989–8

Typeset by Katerprint Typesetting Services, Oxford
Printed in Great Britain by
Cambus Litho Ltd,
East Kilbride, Scotland